# The
# Mermaid
# School

## Series

## Mermaid School

## The Clamshell Show

**Look out for more in the series—coming soon!**

# Mermaid School

Written By
## Lucy Courtenay
## Illustrated By Sheena Dempsey

Amulet Books
New York

Library of Congress Control Number 2019953514

Hardcover ISBN 978-1-4197-4518-8
Paperback ISBN 978-1-4197-4519-5

**ABRAMS** The Art of Books
195 Broadway, New York, NY 10007
abramsbooks.com

For
Mimi,
with love.
L.C.

For
Claire Spillane,
thank you.
S.D.

Pearl's House

Lord Foam's Atoll Academy

Mermaid Lagoon
(Not to scale)

School Rock

LADY SEALIA

Lady Sealia Foam's Mermaid School

Radio Seawave

Marnie's House

N
W E
S

East Lagoon Rocks

Coral Ridge

Clamshell Grotto

"Christabel Loves Arthur" Rock

Orla's House

# Chapter One

It was easy to miss if you didn't know it was there.

"That's the point, Marnie," said her mom. "Lady Sealia doesn't want everyone to know there is a mermaid school in the middle of Mermaid Lagoon."

On the other side of the kitchen table, Marnie's aunt, Christabel, peered over the top of her *Fishtales Monthly* magazine.

"All sorts of strange people could turn up," Aunt Christabel said. "Like me."

Marnie laughed and took another mouthful of Coral Crunch (with seaweed milk) as she gazed out of the cave window at the large pink rock rising in the distance from the lagoon bed. It was hard to tell where the water ended and the rock began.

Today was Marnie's first day at Lady Sealia Foam's Mermaid School, and she had so many questions, she felt like she was going to burst. Was Lady Sealia fierce? What about her deputy, Ms. Mullet? Would she have to ride a seahorse? Would everyone be annoyed or impressed that Marnie's aunt was Christabel Blue, famous singer and radio personality? And most important of all: would she make any friends? That was the part she was really worried about.

"But what is the school like?" she asked.

"Dreadful," said Aunt Christabel.

"Perfectly lovely," said Marnie's mom, at the same time.

Marnie felt anxious. "It can't be both," she said.

"Lady Sealia's is *perfectly lovely*," Marnie's mom repeated. "IF you are good and IF you stick to the rules."

Aunt Christabel lowered her sunglasses. "But Marnie isn't going to do any of those things, I hope," she said. "So it's going to be *dreadful*."

"I *will* do those things," said Marnie firmly. "I'll be the perfect student."

"Pity," said Aunt Christabel.

"You're going to be fine," Marnie told herself as she brushed her long silver-blonde hair after breakfast, and polished her coral pink tail so it gleamed. "No one will care that Christabel Blue is your aunt and you will be NORMAL and FIT IN . . . Oh!" she burst out. "But I do hope I make friends and don't have to ride a seahorse!"

Her mom was waiting by the front door when Marnie returned to the kitchen. Her mom's hair was in an untidy knot on the back of her head, and she had only put one shell earring on this morning. She was so different from Aunt Christabel, it was hard to believe they were sisters.

"It's very important that you make a good impression, Marnie," her mom began. Behind her, Aunt Christabel snorted.

"You won't have much to do with Lady Sealia," her mom continued, "but watch out for Ms. Mullet. She's fair and kind, but very strict."

"She's a silly old crab," said Aunt Christabel, turning the page of her magazine.

"She doesn't like mermaids to be late and she hates it when students forget things," her mom went on. "I once forgot my homework and she wouldn't let me outside to swim at breaktime for three days."

This was the worst thing Marnie's mom had ever done at school. It wasn't very impressive, to be honest.

Marnie wrapped her arms around her fluttery tummy. "I know, Mom," she said. "You've told me a hundred times."

Her mom pushed a loose strand of hair away from Marnie's eyes. "Have you got everything?"

 4

Marnie had a moment of panic. Where was her bag with her shell pens and her seaweed hair bands for gym class? She'd packed it ages ago, and she was sure she had put it beside the cave door last night.

"Looking for this?" asked Aunt Christabel, lifting a shimmering pearl-covered backpack with one of her perfect aqua fingernails.

"Thanks, Auntie," Marnie said with relief. "I packed it days ago. Please can we go now?" *If we don't leave soon,* she thought, *I'll lose my nerve and I'll never go at all.*

But her mom wasn't finished. "One last thing," she

said. "Don't go near the East Lagoon Rocks. Ms. Mullet will tell you all about it, I'm sure, but I've seen for myself the dangers of not listening to her. Your aunt—"

"—sat on the rocks and some humans spotted her and Mermaid Lagoon was almost discovered," Aunt Christabel said. She dropped to the kitchen sofa with a heavy sigh. "If I had a sand dollar for every time I've heard that lecture, I would be rich."

"You ARE rich, Chrissie," said Marnie's mom.

"Is that new, Auntie?" asked Marnie, noticing the large sparkly ring on Christabel's finger.

Aunt Christabel beamed. "Isn't it gorgeous? I love sparkly things," she said. "So does Garbo. Do you know, she stole my crystal mirror the other day? I found it in her bowl. So naughty." She smiled fondly at the snoozing goldfish in her lap. "Just like her mommy."

"I know Aunt Christabel was always in trouble, but I won't be," Marnie said. "I promise."

But her mom's large blue eyes were worried. "Just be careful. You're just like her, you know."

Marnie didn't feel at all like her glamorous aunt. Christabel wasn't scared of making friends or riding seahorses. The only thing they had in common was their singing voices. Marnie's voice was just like Christabel's: high and pure and perfectly in tune. But that was all.

"Christabel never meant to get into trouble, but somehow or other she always did," her mom said. "Your grandpa once got so angry with her that he snapped his trident in half."

"Oh, fishsticks!" said Aunt Christabel. She was now lying full-length on the sofa with Garbo. "Some rules are meant to be broken, and Ms. Mullet was a silly old crab. Still is. I wasn't *that* bad."

Marnie's mom put her hands on her hips. "Singing rude words at the Clamshell Show?"

"A joke!"

"Putting a razor clam in Ms. Mullet's shell purse so that it spat at her when she took out her lipstick? Stealing that school seahorse?"

Through her anxiety, Marnie felt a little stab of relief. She wouldn't steal a seahorse in a million years. She was terrified of them. So she really wasn't like Aunt Christabel at all!

"You've made your point," Aunt Christabel said, rolling her violet eyes toward the cave ceiling. Garbo opened her golden mouth in a perfect O and closed it again. "Marnie,

darling, don't listen to me. Enjoy your first day at school. Be good in all your classes." She gave a naughty grin. "Otherwise you'll turn out fun and gorgeous like me, and not old and boring like your mother."

# Chapter Two

Even close up, School Rock was hard to spot. If Marnie squinted, she could see the place where it broke the surface of Mermaid Lagoon, rippling in the morning light over her head. She clung to her mom with one hand and clutched the strap of her school backpack. She'd never swum this far from the cave before, and it was a little scary.

"Don't steal food from the kitchen," her mom was saying. "Your aunt once stole some oysters from the school garden hoping there were pearls inside. The cook, Monsieur Poisson, was furious!"

"Were there?" asked Marnie, interested. "Pearls inside the oysters?"

"That's not the point," her mom said.

By now, Marnie could see caves and doorways all over School Rock. There were also signs, hanging on seaweed ropes, saying things like OCEANOGRAPHY, SEAHARMONIC ORCHESTRA, and ART STUDIO. It was all so interesting that Marnie forgot to be scared.

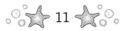

Lady Sealia Foam's
Mermaid School
"Natare, Canare, Esse"

The biggest sign of all hung above a large cave mouth filled with pale blue water and waving plants.

"'*Nature canary essay*,'" Marnie read. "What's a canary?"

"*Natare, canere, esse* means 'Swim, sing, be,'" her mom explained. "It's the school motto. Come along now, we can't be late."

There were other mermaids swimming around them now, with skin and hair and scales in every color, all heading towards Lady Sealia's. Marnie realised no one else was holding hands with their mom.

"I'll be OK now," she said, quickly pulling free. The last thing she needed was for everyone to think she was a baby. "Bye, Mom!"

It felt strange swimming without her mom. Marnie tried to keep up with the other mermaids all moving towards the pale cave with the waving plants, but their tails beat the water and the currents swirled around and it was difficult to swim in a straight line.

"Oh!" she gasped as someone crashed into her.

She caught a glimpse of long black hair and a beautiful rope of pearls.

"Watch where you're going, minnow," snapped the

black-haired mermaid, gliding past with a sweep of a long shiny tail and a flash of blue-purple scales.

"Sorry," said Marnie.

"What are you saying sorry for?" said a voice beside her. "SHE crashed into YOU."

Swimming beside Marnie was a small mermaid with long red hair, glasses, and pale, freckled skin. Her golden scales reminded Marnie of Garbo.

"I'm Pearl Cockle," said the red-haired mermaid. She smiled, showing a gap between her teeth. "Who are you?"

"Marnie Bl—" Marnie stopped. She wasn't sure if she wanted everyone to know her last name yet.

"Pleased to meet you, Marnie Bler," Pearl said. "Are you new?"

Marnie nodded.

"Me too," said Pearl. "Are you scared?"

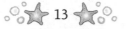 13

Marnie nodded harder.

"Me too," Pearl said again. "But school is just one of those things you have to do, isn't it? If you want to go to college, I mean."

Marnie was impressed. "Do you want to go to college?"

"I'm going to be a marine biologist like my mom. She works in the Indian Ocean a lot of the time." Pearl lifted her chin. "I miss her when she's gone but her work is super-important."

The crowd of mermaids around the pale blue cave mouth with the waving plants was beginning to break up into different lines.

"First years!" called a voice. "Over here please!"

The voice belonged to a large octopus with a chunky coral necklace and a shell-encrusted glasses-case round her neck. She was using all eight of her arms to beckon the first years in the right direction.

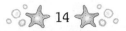

There was a lot of flapping around as everyone tried to line up straight. It was harder than it looked.

"Good morning, first years," said the octopus. "I am Miss Tangle."

"My sister Sheela says hello, Miss Tangle," said someone at the front of the line. "She told me that you were the best teacher she ever had. I'm Orla. Orla Finnegan."

With a sinking heart, Marnie recognized the black-haired mermaid.

"Thank you, Orla," said Miss Tangle warmly. "How is your extremely talented sister?"

"She's doing well, Miss Tangle. She's got a job singing in the Gulf of Mexico."

The first years gasped, and whispered together.

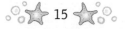

The Gulf of Mexico was famous for its beauty, but also for its dangers. Not many mermaids chose to work there.

"Brave as well as talented, it seems," Miss Tangle said heartily. "How is she coping with the hurricanes and cruise ships?"

Orla's cheeks turned pink. "She doesn't mind them a bit, Miss Tangle."

"What a suck-up," Pearl whispered in Marnie's ear.

Marnie giggled. Miss Tangle gave her a sharp glance and she stopped. She didn't want to get into trouble before she'd even set tail inside the school.

"Into the Assembly Cave now," Miss Tangle said, waving several tentacles. "Lady Sealia will address you all and then take you on your school tour."

Marnie's eyes widened as they all swam into the pale blue cave. It had no roof. They were so close to the surface of Mermaid Lagoon that if Marnie swam up a few feet, she would be able to put her head above the water. There was a wide stage at one end, and the walls were decorated with portraits of the same mermaid, over and over again.

"Lady Sealia must really like having her portrait painted," Pearl whispered to Marnie.

Marnie stared at the long white hair and shimmering

silver-white scales in each portrait. She'd enjoy having her portrait painted too, if she looked as magnificent as Lady Sealia.

The first years swam to a row of coral seats at the base of the stage and sat down.

"Register?" said Miss Tangle, peering around.

A large scallop swam toward the octopus, gracefully opening and closing its fan-shaped shell, and sank into Miss Tangle's outstretched tentacle. The octopus readjusted her glasses on her beak. She peered inside the scallop's shell, where Marnie could see a list of names.

"Dora Agua?" said Miss Tangle.

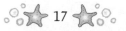

"Here, Miss Tangle," said a brown-haired mermaid with a blue tail.

"Mabel Anemone?"

Next to Pearl, Marnie felt worried. What would happen when everyone heard her last name? Her family were the only Blues in the whole of Mermaid Lagoon.

"Lupita Barracuda?" said Miss Tangle.

Marnie heard a sneeze to her right and turned.

"Do you have a tissue?" Pearl whispered. Her eyes looked red and puffy. "I'm terribly . . . allergic to coral."

Marnie opened her bag to find a tissue for Pearl.

"Marnie Blue?" said Miss Tangle.

At that moment, a bright green sea snake shot out of Marnie's bag. From the look on its face, it hadn't enjoyed being inside there very much. It writhed irritably in the water, tying itself in complicated knots.

"She's got a SNAKE!" someone squealed.

Suddenly everyone started shouting and screaming. Coral chairs fell over and broke on the cave floor, one of Lady Sealia's portraits slid off its hook in the swirling water and disappeared into a bed of seaweed, and the first-year mermaids splashed and squealed and tried to get as far away from Marnie as possible. The snake, meanwhile, untwisted itself and shot off into a dark corner.

"MARNIE BLUE?" repeated Miss Tangle, raising her voice over the chaos.

Marnie put her hand up.

"Here, Miss Tangle," she said in a small voice.

# Chapter Three

Lady Sealia Foam's long white hair was brushed smooth to her head and her scales glimmered in the watery light. She looked older than her portraits, and quite a bit angrier.

Marnie squirmed on her rock chair in front of the headmistress's crystal desk. There was a limpet in the middle of the seat, and it jabbed uncomfortably into her bottom.

This wasn't the way she had wanted to start school at ALL.

"I didn't put the snake in my bag, Lady Sealia," she burst out. "I didn't!"

Lady Sealia narrowed her pale grey eyes. "I hope, Marnie Blue, that we are not planning on acting like this the whole year," she said in a silvery voice that matched her scales.

"No, Lady Sealia," Marnie whispered.

"Dilys is very disappointed," said Lady Sealia.

Marnie stole a glance at Dilys, the dogfish in the corner of the headmistress's crystal-lined study. Dilys didn't look disappointed. Dilys was asleep, her whiskers twitching, probably dreaming of catfish.

"Are you going to tell my mom?" Marnie asked miserably.

Lady Sealia wafted away the question. "Everyone deserves a second chance. But with your . . . unfortunate connections, that second chance is all that you will get."

Marnie gritted her teeth. Why was she related to such a famous troublemaker? *I'm not like my aunt*, she wanted to shout.

"With all the excitement this morning, there is no time left for my usual assembly and tour of the school," Lady Sealia said, admiring herself in the small crystal mirror she was holding. "Ms. Mullet will give it tomorrow instead."

The headmistress set the mirror down, picked up the silvery hairbrush from her crystal desk and started brushing her glowing hair with long, even strokes.

Marnie waited uncertainly.

Lady Sealia lowered her brush. "Why are you still here?"

"Sorry, Lady Sealia," Marnie said hurriedly, backing out of the room. Dilys opened one eye, then closed it again. "Um, bye."

The corridor was full of scallops flapping up and down, delivering messages between classrooms. Pearl was floating outside Lady Sealia's door, ducking whenever a scallop came too close.

"I thought I'd wait for you," she said. "We can go to music class together."

"Thanks," Marnie said.

Pearl glanced at her as they swam down a long corridor. "Everyone is saying your aunt is Christabel Blue," she said with interest. "Is it true?"

"I guess." Marnie wasn't in the mood to talk about Aunt Christabel.

"That's amazing!" Pearl's eyes were bright. "I'm her biggest fan. What's she like in real life?"

Marnie shrugged. "Like she is on Radio SeaWave. Funny, and always singing. But she sleeps a lot. And she's always teasing my mom. And she talks to her pet fish."

"That's so cool," Pearl gasped.

Marnie felt a little glimmer of pride. Maybe being related to Christabel Blue wasn't ALL bad. Except when she put snakes in your school bag for fun.

Marnie had been looking forward to her music lessons. But the way Miss Tangle was looking at her, music lessons weren't going to be any fun at all.

"There's no need to ask who *you're* related to," said Miss Tangle with a sniff. "I had hoped with a mother like yours you would be a sensible, hardworking member of my class. But after this morning's performance, it's clear that you take after another member of your family."

Marnie tried to smile. "Did you teach my mom, Miss Tangle?"

"I had the pleasure of teaching your mother, yes." Miss Tangle frowned. "I also taught your aunt Christabel." She looked like she was eating rotten seaweed as she said Christabel's name. "I judge my pupils on how many tentacles I need to keep them under control," she went on. "And Christabel Blue was a ten-tentacle sort of pupil."

"But you've only got eight tentacles, Miss Tangle," said Pearl.

"Exactly," said Miss Tangle, with some force. "I'm watching you, Marnie Blue. Sit down."

"Sit with me, Marnie!" said Lupita Barracuda, a bright-eyed mermaid with a cloud of deep brown curly hair and glimmering black scales. "You can have a minnow chew if you like."

"I just love your aunt," sighed Dora Agua, the mermaid with the blue tail. "Can I have her autograph?"

"This is a music lesson," said Miss Tangle loudly. "Not a Christabel Blue fan club."

Marnie sank down on a rock at the back of the cave and tried to become invisible.

"Now," said Miss Tangle, when everyone had quietened down. "I'm sure you don't need me to tell you the importance of singing in a mermaid's education."

"It's very important indeed, Miss Tangle," said a familiar voice at the front of the class.

It was the black-haired mermaid again. Orla, with the super-talented sister in the Gulf of Mexico. Pearl rolled her eyes at Marnie, who felt a little better.

Miss Tangle beamed. "You're right, Orla. Mermaids have used their singing voices for thousands of years. They have lured human ships onto rocks, it's true. But they have also lured them *away* from rocks. You all know the danger you mermaids would be in if humans ever found out about you, but that doesn't mean you should wish them harm. Humans are a threat, but not an enemy. It's a simple matter of staying hidden."

"Yes, Miss Tangle," said Orla. She looked at Marnie coldly. "Mermaids who nearly get us discovered are a real menace."

Marnie felt her cheeks going red. Everyone in Mermaid Lagoon knew the story of Christabel and the East Lagoon Rocks. Orla was clearly talking about her aunt.

"Indeed," Miss Tangle agreed, with a hard stare at Marnie. "Now let's see what sort of voices we have in this class."

"Oh dear," said Pearl.

Marnie glanced at her. "Don't you like singing?"

"I like it very much," said Pearl sadly. "But singing doesn't like ME."

"There will be two groups," said Miss Tangle, drifting around the music cave with her tentacles trailing and her coral beads clinking. "The first group will sing the words to the song and practice keeping their voices clear but full of charm. The second group will focus on harmonies, working on their tone and volume."

Orla was put in the first group.

"Dora Agua and Pearl Cockle?" said Miss Tangle. "Join Orla please."

Pearl looked worried. "Marnie, will you help me? If your aunt is Christabel Blue, I bet you're really good."

"I'll help you if Miss Tangle puts me in the first group," promised Marnie.

Miss Tangle narrowed her eyes. "Marnie Blue? Second group."

Marnie made an apologetic face at Pearl, who made a face back.

"Harmonizing is an important life skill for a mermaid," said Miss Tangle to the second group.

Marnie was determined not to be a diva like Aunt Christabel. "I'll do my best, Miss Tangle," she said.

Miss Tangle looked a little more approving. "Follow the harmonies now. *Ocean blue, ocean true, waves to make the world anew . . .*"

"*Ocean blue . . .*" sang the mermaids in the first group. "*Ocean true . . .*"

"*La, la, la,*" sang Marnie in the second group, trying not to mind that she wasn't singing the pretty tune or the lovely words.

"*OcEEAN blOOO,*" sang Pearl.

Marnie winced. Pearl was as flat as a flounder.

"Miss Tangle?" Orla complained. "Pearl Cockle sounds like a boiled catfish. She's messing the rest of us up."

Pearl blushed as the other mermaids giggled.

"Perhaps you could sit this one out, Pearl," Miss Tangle said. "Do I have any volunteers to take Pearl's place?"

Marnie put her hand up so high that she almost touched the roof of the cave. "Please, Miss Tangle," she said a little breathlessly. "Can I sing the tune?"

"She'll be so good, Miss Tangle," Pearl said at once.

Marnie gave her a grateful glance. Miss Tangle sighed.

"Very well," she said. "But if you show off, or do anything silly . . ."

"I won't!" said Marnie. "I promise!"

As Miss Tangle raised her tentacles, Marnie threw herself joyfully into singing the tune, letting the words and sounds roll around her. She forgot where she was and whom she was singing with. Which turned out to be a mistake.

"Excuse me, Miss Tangle?" came a voice.

Still holding her highest note, Marnie opened her eyes. She was the only person in the room who was still singing.

"Marnie Blue's showing off," said Orla with a toss of her long black hair.

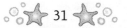

Marnie wished she could disappear into the rock floor.

Miss Tangle glared. "Marnie Blue! This is an ensemble class, not a solo performance!"

"Miss Tangle, I wasn't, I—"

"I had enough of that behavior from your aunt," said Miss Tangle furiously. "I won't put up with it from you as well. Out of my class! Now!"

Marnie swam out, trying not to cry.

# Chapter
## Four

"So how was school?"

Silently Marnie helped herself to sea anemone juice.

Her mom tried again. "Did you have a good day?"

Marnie shrugged and drank her juice in one gulp.

"You're like a tiger shark with toothache," Aunt Christabel said. "What happened?"

Marnie was determined not to cry. "It was a horrible day and I DON'T WANT TO TALK ABOUT IT."

She swam out of the kitchen and into her room, threw herself down on her clamshell bed and pressed her face into the sea-moss pillow.

She wished she'd never started Mermaid School.

What was the point, if she was going to get into trouble all the time?

Her door opened. Aunt Christabel swam in with Garbo tucked under her arm.

"You should have knocked," Marnie said, angry now as well as upset.

"I never knock," said Aunt Christabel. "It's the secret of my success." She sat on the end of Marnie's clamshell bed. "So, what happened at school today?"

"*You* should know," said Marnie furiously. "You started it."

Christabel looked startled. "What did *I* do?"

Marnie looked her aunt straight in the eye. "You put that sea snake in my bag!"

Aunt Christabel let Garbo go. "I have no idea what you're talking about," she said as the little goldfish swam around the cave, sniffing the sea flowers on the rocky walls.

Marnie glared. "I was looking for my bag this morning and you gave it to me and the next thing I know there's a stinky sea snake inside that swims out and scares everyone and gets me into trouble!"

Aunt Christabel looked thoughtful. "And you think I put it in there?"

"I had to go and see Lady Sealia!" Marnie wailed. "I got a warning because you're my aunt! I'm trying to be *me*, Aunt Christabel, and the only thing anyone talked about all day was how I was just like *you* because I was so naughty. And I'm NOT and now I don't want to go back to Mermaid School EVER."

Christabel reached over and brushed Marnie's tears away with her thumb. "Slow down, minnow," she said. "I didn't put anything in your bag. Why would I?"

"Because you thought it would be funny!"

Aunt Christabel raised a perfect eyebrow. "There is a difference between playing a prank and being mean, Marnie. I may be many things, but I'm not mean."

Marnie suddenly felt uncertain. She wanted to believe her aunt. But if Christabel hadn't put the snake in her bag, then who had?

*Minnow.*

A memory tickled the back of Marnie's mind. Someone else had called her a minnow today.

*Watch where you're going, minnow.*

"Orla Finnegan!" Marnie gasped. "She bumped into me on the way to school AND she's been horrible to me all day. Maybe it was her!" She felt confused. "But why would she be picking on me? I don't even know her."

Aunt Christabel clicked her tongue at Garbo, who swam back into her arms. "Enemies move in mysterious

ways," she said. "Like octopuses. Octopuses swim
backward, did you know?"

Marnie didn't. She rubbed her nose. "My teacher Miss
Tangle is an octopus," she said. "She's another one who
thinks I'm naughty like you were."

"I'll tell you a secret about Miss Tangle," said Aunt
Christabel, tickling Garbo's chin. "When she farts, she
shoots out ink."

Marnie gave a startled giggle.

Aunt Christabel smiled. "So, those are the enemies you made today. What about the friends?"

Marnie thought about the little gap in Pearl's teeth when she smiled. "Pearl Cockle's nice," she said, feeling better. "Lupita Barracuda and Dora Agua seem OK too, although I think they just want your autograph."

"They sound very sensible," said Aunt Christabel. "Three friends and one enemy then, not counting teachers. I think we know who's winning."

Marnie threw her arms around her aunt. "Thank you," she said into Aunt Christabel's shoulder. "You always know the right thing to say."

Aunt Christabel rubbed Marnie's back. "Come and have dinner. It'll make you feel better."

In the kitchen, Marnie's mom was stirring something on a large hot-water vent that stuck up from the lagoon bed.  The shell pan popped and bubbled, releasing lovely smells, and Marnie realized how hungry she was. She gave her mom an impulsive hug as they sat down to large bowls of kelp casserole.

"Sorry I was weird earlier," she said. "It was a rough day."

"Tomorrow will be better, I'm sure," said her mom. Marnie felt her mood dip again. Tomorrow would still have Orla in it. And Pearl, she reminded herself. And Lupita and Dora. But Orla's mean face stayed in her mind.

"Mom," she said as they cleared the table after dinner. "What should I do if someone doesn't like me?"

Her mom stopped stacking the shell bowls in the hot-vent dishwasher. "Someone at school doesn't like you?" she said. "Who?"

"No one," said Marnie quickly. "I just want to know what to do."

"Be nice to them," her mom said anxiously. "When someone is mean, there's usually something making them sad."

Marnie screwed up her face. Being nice to Orla would be hard.

"What do you think?" she asked, turning to her aunt.

"Stay out of their way," Aunt Christabel advised. "And don't let them see that you're scared." She glanced at the arms on the starfish clock that clung to the kitchen wall. "Neptune's knickers, is that the time? I'm going to be late for my show!"

As she brushed her hair that night, Marnie thought about her mom and Christabel's advice. It was nice that they were trying to help, but they didn't have to face Orla in the morning. Marnie was going to worry all night and not get any sleep.

"Would you like a Queen Maretta story?" her mom asked when she came in to tuck Marnie up. "To take your mind off things?"

"Yes please," Marnie said gratefully. She'd been feeling a bit too grown-up for stories lately, but tonight it was just what she needed.

Her mom clapped her hands. "Go and find your dinner, Horace," she said.

The large angler fish swimming slowly around Marnie's ceiling switched off his dangling light and swam out of the room. Now Marnie's room was lit only by the pinpricks of light from the tiny phosphorescent fish that lived in the walls.

"When Maretta was Queen of the Merfolk, there was a terrible storm," her mom began. "The coral reefs and lagoon caves broke into pieces. The waters were so rough that the fish disappeared. The merfolk were going to starve if Maretta didn't do something. So she went in search of the Weathermaker.

"Everyone knew the Weathermaker was a bully who liked nothing better than sending bad weather to Mermaid Lagoon. But even the Weathermaker had never sent a storm this terrible. Maretta battled through the waves to the furthest shores of the lagoon, over to the caves where the Weathermaker lived above the surface.

"'Weathermaker!' she called from the wild water. 'I want to talk to you!'

"'I'm not leaving my cave,' came the Weathermaker's grumpy reply. 'You'll have to come to ME.'

"Maretta knew that if she left the water, she would have to give up her voice in exchange for human legs. But her people were counting on her, and she didn't hesitate. She left the lagoon and walked on dry land to the mouth of the Weathermaker's cave."

"What's it like?" Marnie interrupted, fascinated. "Having legs?"

"I've never been brave enough to find out," said her mom.

"Do you always have to give up your voice in order to have legs?" Marnie asked. "What if you never get it back? And what about your tail? Do you always get your tail back when you go into the water again?"

"I don't know," said her mom. "Now, Maretta walked up to the Weathermaker's cave, ready to have an argument. But to her surprise, the Weathermaker was crying.

"'No one likes me,' he sobbed. 'No one ever visits me in my cave. I don't have any friends!'

"Maretta forgot her anger and put her arm around the Weathermaker instead. The Weathermaker was cold and rigid, but Maretta hugged him until he started warming up. And as he warmed up, the sun came out and the waves quietened. The storm was over. Maretta had saved her people, and Mermaid Lagoon was calm again."

Marnie snuggled deeper into her sea-moss covers and yawned. The Weathermaker just wanted a friend, she thought as she floated away to sleep. But she couldn't imagine risking her voice and her tail to make friends with Orla. No way.

# Chapter
## Five

The mermaids wriggled in their coral seats, listening to the deputy head speaking from the rocky stage. Pearl sneezed five times in a row and Marnie gave her a tissue. Her ears burned with the effort of not looking at Orla.

Ms. Mullet's voice echoed around the Assembly Cave. Her shell glittered with tiny barnacles and her small eyes swivelled on their stalks. Marnie had a feeling that the old crab missed nothing. There was no sign of Lady Sealia, except in the portraits on the walls.

". . . and please remember not to chase the reef sharks," Ms. Mullet was saying. "They can be unpredictable, particularly at lunchtime . . . I'm pleased to say that the library is open again after this  morning's unfortunate snapper invasion. Thank you, Len."

A brown-and-white-striped lionfish sitting to one side

of the stage looked up from his book, lazily waved his frilled fins, and looked down again.

Pearl leaned in to Marnie. "Lionfish are really venomous," she whispered. "I feel sorry for the snapper . . . ATCHOO! Can I have another tissue?"

A small grey fish flapped up to Ms. Mullet and whispered something.

". . . and Monsieur Poisson asks that no one enter the sea cucumber patch as our sea cucumbers are breeding. They taste funny if they've been disturbed," Ms. Mullet finished. She snapped her claws. "Now, as you are aware, yesterday's tour of the school did not take place."

"And we all know whose fault that was," Marnie heard Orla whisper to Mabel Anemone a few seats away.

"I will lead the tour right after this assembly." Ms. Mullet's eyes swivelled in the direction of the first years. "Every first year is to gather outside the Assembly Cave and wait for me there. Thank you for your attention."

Marnie waited until Orla had swept out of the Assembly Cave in front of her. She didn't want to give the black-haired mermaid another chance to play a trick on her. But apart from a dirty look, Orla ignored Marnie completely.

"I think Orla put that snake in my bag yesterday," Marnie told Pearl as they swam out of the cave for Ms. Mullet's tour. "She wanted me to get into trouble."

"Why?" asked Pearl.

Marnie shook her head. "I don't know. But it's the only theory I've got."

"Attention please."

Ms. Mullet was perched on a ledge above the first years, who stopped chattering at once.

"Welcome to Lady Sealia Foam's Mermaid School," said the deputy head. "The school was set up by Lady Sealia's great-great-great grandmother, Queen Maretta, to prepare young mermaids for life in the Seven Seas."

This made the first years chatter all over again. They

had been listening to stories about Queen Maretta all their lives. Marnie thought about her mom's story last night. It was amazing to think Queen Maretta was once alive.

"All our classrooms, laboratories, kitchens, stables and library are built into School Rock," Ms. Mullet continued, "all the way from the surface of the lagoon to the bottom of the seabed. Follow me."

As Ms. Mullet scuttled away, the first years followed with a swish of their tails.

"Where do the merboys go to school?" Dora Agua wanted to know.

"Atoll Academy, on the other side of the lagoon," said Pearl. "Lady Sealia's husband Lord Foam runs it."

"How do *you* know that, flounder-face?" said Orla, making Mabel Anemone laugh.

"I just do," Pearl said, tilting her chin. "And I don't have a face like a flounder, actually, because flounders have eyes on top of their heads and I don't."

Pearl was brave, talking back to Orla like that. Braver than Marnie. *But that's not difficult*, Marnie thought gloomily.

"Keep up, first years!" came Ms. Mullet's voice.

The Music Department was one level down from Lady Sealia's office and the Assembly Cave. Marnie's thoughts drifted as Ms. Mullet took them past the practice rooms and classrooms where Marnie had spent most of yesterday sitting in the corridor. She was taken by surprise when Orla barged into her, causing Marnie to scrape her tail painfully on the wall.

"Clumsy," said Orla, narrowing her eyes.

Marnie tried to be as brave as Pearl. "I'm not clumsy," she squeaked. "You are."

"I didn't do anything," said Orla, folding her arms.

"Yes you did," said Marnie a little desperately.

". . . our Seaharmonic Orchestra is always looking for members, particularly players of the rock tuba and razor-clam flute," Ms. Mullet was saying. "If anyone is interested, please see Miss Tangle. On we go."

Orla flipped her tail and shot away down the rocky corridor with Mabel Anemone. Marnie swam slowly after the others.

 51

"What did Orla say?" Pearl asked as they swam past the Oceanography Cave with its large observation window.

"Nothing," Marnie muttered.

"Orla's mean, isn't she?" said Dora.

"Especially to Marnie," Lupita agreed.

"Everyone's noticed."

"I reckon she's jealous that Marnie's related to Christabel," said Pearl.

Marnie hadn't thought of that.

Dora and Lupita agreed, and then started discussing their favorite Christabel Blue songs.

"I like 'Wave Goodbye.'"

"'Clamshell Heart' is better."

"She's so funny on Radio SeaWave," said Dora, giggling.

"And she has the most amazing clothes in those fashion shoots she does for *Fishtales Monthly*," sighed Lupita. "Marnie, can we meet her one day? Please?"

"Sure," said Marnie absently. She was still thinking about what Pearl had said. Could jealousy really be the reason Orla was so mean to her? It seemed very strange.

Like the Oceanography Cave, the Art Studio had large windows to let in as much light as possible.

In the library, the books in their dark blue mussel-shell cases were lined up on rocky shelves as neatly as the stripes on Len the lionfish librarian's fins.

"You can borrow as many books as you like," Ms. Mullet told them. "Just be sure to put them back where you found them, or Len will have something to say."

"I think it's disgusting, having a poisonous librarian," Mabel Anemone said as they swam on down the rock. "I'm never going in the library."

"Lionfish are venomous," said Pearl. "Not poisonous."

Mabel rolled her eyes at Orla. "Like that even matters?"

"You can eat venomous fish," said Pearl. "You can't eat poisonous ones."

"Good to know for when we eat the librarian," said Orla sarcastically.

The deeper they swam, the darker it became. They passed the Sports Caves with their fishball nets and weightlifting equipment. ("The

pressure of the water at this level ensures a good workout.")
The Dance Studio had a barre made out of a wrecked
ship's mast and polished crystal mirrors lining the walls.

"And now the stables," Ms. Mullet said, pointing at
a series of craggy oyster-shell half-doors near the bottom
of School Rock.

Marnie drew back. She had never liked seahorses, with
their bony heads and sharp teeth. How Aunt Christabel
had been brave enough to steal one was beyond her.

Orla noticed her expression. "Is Marnie Blue *scared*?"
she said with interest. She swam closer to one of the stable
doors, holding out her hand. "Come on, little seahorse,"
she said. "Show us your fangs."

"Come away from there please," Ms. Mullet said
sharply. "Seahorses bite. The stable master, Mr. Splendid,
is away this morning, and has asked that no one enters the
stables until he returns." She snapped her claws to keep
the first years' attention. "Now, the last place to see is
on the seabed itself. The hot-water vents are used by our
laboratories, Domestic Science Department and school
kitchens. No dawdling please."

"I dare you to go inside a stable," Orla whispered in
Marnie's ear as Ms. Mullet swam off around the corner.

"I don't want to," said Marnie.

"Why? Is the famous Marnie Blue scared?" sneered Orla. Beside her, Mabel snickered.

Marnie's heart bounced around her chest like a frightened prawn. She gulped, remembering Aunt Christabel's advice: *Don't let them see that you're scared.*

"OK. I'll do it if you will," she found herself saying.

# Chapter Six

Orla's eyes flickered. "Fine," she said. "After you."

Dora and Lupita hung back with Pearl and Mabel as Marnie put her hand on the latch of the nearest stable door.

"What if Ms. Mullet comes back?" said Mabel nervously. "We'll get into trouble."

"This won't take long, Mabel," said Orla. "Marnie's too scared to go through with it anyway."

"She'll do it," said Pearl at once. "You wait."

Marnie wished Pearl wasn't so supportive. She *had* to do it now.

She made herself look over the top of the stable door. Small phosphorescent fish swam about, filling the dark stable with a faint glow of light. A large pair of eyes glared at her. Before she could change her mind, Marnie opened the stable door and went inside.

The seahorse screamed. It beat its scarlet fins and tail and reared, churning the water into a froth. It bared its teeth and snapped at her in rage. Marnie shrieked and stumbled, falling backward out of the stable.

"Shut the door!"

"It's going crazy, don't let it out!"

Pearl, Dora and Lupita rushed to shut the stable door before the seahorse escaped. It took all three of them to hold the door shut while Marnie fixed the latch back into place. Her fingers felt like jellyfish. There was no sign of Orla or Mabel.

"MARNIE BLUE!"

Marnie whirled around. Ms. Mullet was scuttling towards them with her claws raised. Behind her, clustered with the rest of the first years, were Orla Finnegan and Mabel Anemone.

"What did I say about not entering the stables?" Ms. Mullet's eyes swivelled furiously as the seahorse roared and bucked and kicked at the stable door. "Mr. Splendid will be extremely angry that you have upset his animals. Thank Neptune that Orla and Mabel had the good sense to warn me about what you were doing. Detention this afternoon!"

"It wasn't Marnie's fault, Ms. Mullet," Pearl said, looking furiously at Orla. The black-haired mermaid dipped her eyes. "It was—"

"I saw Marnie coming out of that stable, Pearl Cockle," interrupted Ms. Mullet. "Report to Mr. Splendid after lunch, Marnie. And count yourself lucky that I don't send a warning scallop to your parents."

The deputy head swept away with Orla, Mabel and the other first years, muttering something that sounded suspiciously like "Just like her aunt." Orla didn't look back.

"Orla said she'd go into the stable, but she told on you instead?" Dora gasped.

Lupita folded her arms. "I'm never talking to Orla Finnegan again."

"Are you OK, Marnie?" Pearl asked.

Marnie was surprised to find that she was fine. Maybe it was Orla's moment of uncertainty when Marnie had challenged her. Or maybe it was because Dora, Lupita, and Pearl had all stood up for her. Either way, she felt stronger than she'd ever felt before.

"Yes," she said. "Honestly. Don't worry about me."

Marnie swam down to the stables after lunch for her detention, wondering what kind of creature Mr. Splendid was. She wished Orla had dared her to go into Monsieur Poisson's sea cucumber patch instead. A detention in the school's kitchen garden would probably have been OK.

"Hello?" she called nervously. "Mr. Splendid? I'm Marnie Blue and I've come—"

A flash of yellow caught her eye. A magnificent toadfish was swimming slowly towards her, waving his long purple-spotted tail from side to side and beating his frilly yellow fins. If this was Mr. Splendid, he was very splendid indeed.

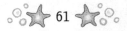

"Marnie Blue, you say?" said the toadfish in a deep voice. "Any relation to Christabel?"

Marnie sighed. "Yes, Mr. Splendid, but I'm not like my aunt at all, I—"

"Lovely girl, Christabel," said Mr. Splendid fondly. "Excellent with my seahorses. Particularly Urchin. Urchin never let anyone else ride him but your aunt. How is she?"

Marnie stared. "She's fine. Thanks."

Mr. Splendid swam majestically towards a stable door. "I listen to her show, of course," he said, lifting the latch. "Never miss it. Come along then, Marnie Blue. These stables won't clean themselves."

This was the first teacher Marnie had met who actually

*liked* Christabel. She followed the toadfish cautiously, listening to Mr. Splendid talking to the seahorse inside.

"Sandy, my dear. We have a visitor to clean you up today. Try not to bite."

Sandy snapped her jaws once or twice as Marnie took the stable brush and started clearing up the manure on the rocky floor of the stable. It smelled worse than Garbo's, and there was a lot more of it.

"Monsieur Poisson will fetch it later for the kitchen gardens," said Mr. Splendid. "Marvelous fertilizer for his sea roses."

Marnie grimly swept and scrubbed and ducked away from the seahorses" darting teeth. She didn't like their

googly eyes or their hard, ridged bodies. Although she was enjoying Mr. Splendid's stories of Aunt Christabel as she worked.

"Never seen such a fine rider. She used to race Urchin from the top of School Rock to the bottom, and no one could ever catch her. She took him out a few times without permission too." The toadfish smiled at the memory. "Not one for rules, your aunt."

"Oh, I know," said Marnie.

The next seahorse was Andrew.

"I can't for the life of me remember why we called him that," said Mr. Splendid as Marnie tried to sweep up the manure from under Andrew's long, curled green tail. "Good boy, Andrew."

Finally they reached the angry seahorse's stable.

"You'd better let me clean out Typhoon," advised Mr. Splendid. "We don't want to deliver you back to Ms. Mullet in pieces. Typhoon was the one you decided to visit this morning, wasn't he?"

Marnie flushed and nodded.

"I don't imagine you'll be visiting him again without permission," said Mr. Splendid with a slow grin. "Or with permission either. Typhoon's tricky."

The toadfish swam into the stable and came out again

a few minutes later with a shovel of manure and the clear outline of a bite on one of his yellow fins. He dumped the manure outside the door as Typhoon screamed in defiance, and handed the shovel back to Marnie.

"Right," he said. "Just Urchin left."

A low growling noise was coming from the stable door at the end of the row. Marnie hadn't noticed it on the tour.

"You said Urchin only let Christabel ride him," she said, feeling uneasy as the growling continued. "Is he like Typhoon?"

"Oh much worse," said Mr. Splendid cheerfully. "No one dares to ride him these days. But he won't bite a Blue. I'm sure of it." He paused. "Quite sure, anyway."

Gripping the shovel for courage, Marnie peered inside the growling stable. At first, she could see nothing. Then suddenly, a long, bony blue face loomed over the top of the stable door, jaws wide and teeth on display. Marnie flinched backward.

"Hold steady," Mr. Splendid said. "He's just having a sniff."

Marnie squeezed her eyes shut, feeling the gentle whiffling of the water as Urchin sniffed her. *Please don't bite me. Please . . .*

Something hard settled on her shoulder. She opened one eye, hardly daring to breathe as the seahorse snuffled and pushed against her.

"Told you," said Mr. Splendid in satisfaction. "You smell like a Blue. Give him a scratch and he'll be your friend forever."

Marnie cautiously put up a hand and scratched Urchin between his wide, bulgy eyes. The seahorse made a purring sound and fluttered his pale blue fins.

"There you go, you old devil," said Mr. Splendid. "You can let Marnie clean out your stable now."

# Chapter
## Seven

Marnie swam to oceanography, thinking about Urchin. It was amazing that he had recognised her because she smelled like her aunt. She couldn't wait to tell Christabel.

"Marnie!" Pearl was waving from the Oceanography Cave.

"Mr. Scampi says a large school of blue tang is about to swim past. Come on! We saved you a seat."

Dora and Lupita grinned at Marnie and beckoned her over to the big observation window.

Mabel Anemone was sitting alone at the front of the class. Marnie looked around for Orla, but couldn't see her.

"What did I miss?" Marnie asked, swimming up to her friends.

"Just some boring stuff about ocean weather," said Lupita.

"The good part's about to begin," said Pearl eagerly. "We have to count the blue tang when we see them."

A large black lobster at the front of the classroom waggled his claws at her. "Marnie Blue?" he said.

"Sorry I'm late," said Marnie quickly, taking a seaweed scroll and shell pen out of her backpack. She hoped Mr. Scampi wasn't another one of the teachers who hated her aunt.

Mr. Scampi flicked his antennae. "Take a seat and start counting."

Marnie had barely sat down when there was a flicker of color outside the window. The mermaids gasped. A rippling wave of bright blue fish glided past, their fins glowing with color.

"Onetwothreefourfive," Pearl said very quickly. "Sixseveneight . . ."

The room filled with the sound of counting voices.

"Tang are extremely poisonous," Mr. Scampi said, raising his voice over the noise. "You are strongly advised never to eat one."

"What's the difference between venomous and poisonous again, Pearl?" asked Lupita.

"Shh," said Pearl, cross-eyed with the effort of counting the tang. "Seventeeneighteennineteen . . ."

"You can eat venomous fish but not poisonous ones," said Dora. "I think."

Marnie counted twenty-five tang and then lost her place. "Where's Orla?" she asked Lupita, who had given up at eleven.

"Don't know, don't care," said Lupita.

"No one talked to her at lunch, Marnie," Dora said, leaning in close. "Not even Mabel. Orla sat down at a table and everyone else left. Imagine!"

"Nobody likes a tattletail," said Lupita darkly.

"Orla Finnegan is a tattletail AND a liar AND a scaredy catfish for not going in the stable after you like she said she would."

"Thirtythreethirtyfourthirtyfive," said Pearl.

Marnie felt guilty. She didn't like the thought of anyone sitting alone in the Dining Cave. Not even Orla Finnegan.

"But lunch was ages ago," she said. "Why isn't she in class?"

"Fifty-three!" Pearl shouted as the last tang swept past. Everyone else had stopped counting. "There were fifty-three, Mr. Scampi."

"Excellent," said Mr. Scampi. "Write it down."

Lupita wrote "fifty-three" in large curly letters on her seaweed scroll. "Good riddance to bad oysters," she said. "I don't care if I never see Orla Finnegan again."

Marnie invited Pearl, Dora, and Lupita back for dinner after school, but only Pearl could come. The others made Marnie promise to invite them another time, and swam home reluctantly in the opposite direction.

"Don't you think it's weird that Orla wasn't around this afternoon?" said Marnie as she and Pearl skimmed

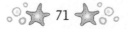

along, enjoying the feel of the cool water on their tails. "So far, she's usually sat at the front and sucked up to teachers. Even with everyone giving her the silent treatment, she wouldn't skip class."

"She was there for the start of oceanography, when Mr. Scampi was talking about that hurricane," Pearl said. "I saw her by herself at the back."

"What hurricane?" said Marnie.

"Oh! I forgot you missed that part," said Pearl.

"There's this really bad hurricane that's just struck the Gulf of Mexico. Force nine, Mr. Scampi was saying."

"The Gulf of Mexico?" said Marnie. "Orla's sister works in the Gulf of Mexico."

Pearl looked puzzled. "Oh yes. I forgot that. But why are you worried? I thought you hated Orla."

"Orla hates me," Marnie pointed out. "Not the other way around."

Marnie was scared of Orla, but she didn't hate her. Marnie wasn't the hating type.

"I'm sooo nervous about meeting your aunt," Pearl confessed.

Marnie pulled her thoughts away from Orla. "She'll make you laugh as soon as you meet her, I promise," she said. "Want to race there?"

Pearl flipped her golden tail and took off. Laughing, Marnie chased her. They ducked through the seaweed and dodged the little shoals of fish, and Pearl sneezed when she got too close to the coral reef.

Suddenly Marnie stopped and cocked her head. She could hear crying. Leaving Pearl practicing somersaults on the lagoon bed, she swam to an outcrop of coral and looked behind it cautiously.

Orla Finnegan's eyes were as red as the coral she was

sitting on. Crouching with her arms wrapped around her tail, she glared at Marnie.

"This is your aunt's fault," she spat. "It's ALL HER FAULT!"

Marnie struggled to understand what Orla was talking about. "I'm so sorry," she said, her thoughts scattering like bubbles. "I don't—"

Orla reared up like Typhoon the seahorse. "She didn't play my sister's song on Radio SeaWave." Her

voice was as cold as an Arctic current. "She promised to play it. She PROMISED. Sheela was going to launch her singing career in Mermaid Lagoon. But instead she had to go to the Gulf of Mexico for work and now she's missing in the hurricane! Your aunt's a liar. I hate her and I hate YOU!"

And with a sob and a flip of her long purple tail, she swam away.

## Chapter Eight

"So Orla hates you because your aunt didn't play her sister's music on her radio show?" said Pearl. "That's crazy!"

"I know," said Marnie. "But that's what she said."

Pearl helped herself to an algae cracker from the shell plate on Marnie's kitchen table. "So what are you going to do?" she mumbled through a mouthful.

"Have your dinner," advised Marnie's mom, who was cooking starfish fritters on the cave's hot vents. "You can't make plans on an empty stomach."

Aunt Christabel breezed through the door in a beautiful blue sea-moss coat, with Garbo on a crystal-studded lead.

"Do I smell starfish fritters?" she said.

"And waveberry pie for pudding," said Marnie's mom. "Good food is very important for growing brains."

"My brain stopped growing years ago," said Aunt Christabel, letting Garbo off her lead.

"Auntie, this is my friend Pearl Cockle," said Marnie.

Pearl turned bright pink as she shook Christabel's hand. Marnie had that strange feeling again: the one where she understood that her aunt meant something completely different to other people.

"So, tell me, Pearl Cockle," said Aunt Christabel as they settled down to eat. "Is my niece being very naughty at school and keeping up the family name?"

"Marnie's not naughty at all," Pearl said shyly. Her cheeks were still pink. "Her detention at lunch was completely unfair."

"Detention?" gasped Marnie's mom with horror.

"Detention?" said Aunt Christabel with interest, at exactly the same time. "What did she do?"

"It's a long story," said Marnie, passing the starfish fritters to Pearl.

"The interesting stories always are," said Aunt Christabel. "Go to your bowl, Garbo," she instructed her goldfish, who was lurking by her chair. "Begging is very unattractive."

Marnie started telling her mom and aunt about Orla, and Orla's sister Sheela, and Mr. Splendid, and Urchin.

"Dear Urchin!" Aunt Christabel exclaimed, clapping her hands. The anglerfish on the kitchen ceiling switched on and off in confusion. "You must give him fifty kisses and a handful of krill treats from me next time you see him, Marnie."

"I don't like the sound of this Orla person," Marnie's mom said.

"She's just worried about her sister," said Marnie. "When you're worried, I think you do ridiculous things."

Marnie didn't know what she'd do if her mom or Aunt Christabel disappeared. She felt sick just thinking about it.

"My mom was almost caught in a tsunami in the Indian Ocean last year," Pearl said. "Dad and I were so worried that we forgot to bring in the fish for the night and they all escaped. We had to eat algae for a few days until Dad rounded them up again."

Marnie took a sip from her sea anemone juice. "So you don't remember Sheela Finnegan's demo, Auntie?" she asked.

"I get a lot of demos, Marnie," Aunt Christabel said.

"Orla said you promised to play it," Marnie persisted.

A puzzled look crossed Aunt Christabel's face. "Finnegan? Tall girl, dark hair, purple tail?"

"Sounds like Orla," said Marnie.

"Yes," agreed Pearl.

"I remember now!" Aunt Christabel exclaimed. "I was going to play it, but the demo disappeared."

"How can a demo disappear?" asked Marnie.

Aunt Christabel sighed. "I've lost all sorts of things in the studio lately. To be fair, the place is a mess. I need an assistant to sort it all out." She checked her wrist and tutted. "Garbo? Have you taken my watch?"

The goldfish looked up guiltily from her bowl. The sparkly links on Christabel's tiny starfish watch gleamed on her sea-moss bed.

"Why don't you and Pearl come with me to the studio after dinner, Marnie?" suggested Aunt Christabel as she scooped up her watch. "Take a look for yourselves? You can listen to the recording while you're at it."

Pearl gasped. "We can actually watch you recording the show? That is *off the reef*!"

"I'll even give you a shout-out if you like," said Christabel, taking a slice of waveberry pie and popping it into her mouth.

"I'm so glad I met you, Marnie," Pearl sighed. "This is the best day ever!"

The Radio SeaWave studio was only a few starfish seconds away from Marnie's house. Pearl chattered to Christabel the whole way about her favorite songs and parts of the show while Garbo chased tiny fish and zoomed in and out of the water weed.

"I like the 'Love Underwater' section best, but Dad likes 'Dance 'n' Dazzle,'" Pearl told Christabel. "Mom loves the show too when she's home, but she works away in the Indian Ocean a lot."

"Marnie's dad works away too," said Christabel.

"He mines natural gas in the Atlantic," Marnie explained to Pearl. "He's been away since I was four. I don't think about him very much, to be honest."

"I gave my poor dad so much trouble," Christabel

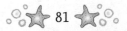

sighed. "It amazes me that he didn't swim off to the Atlantic as well."

"Did you really swim all the way to the East Lagoon Rocks when you were at school?" Pearl asked eagerly.

"Yes," Christabel said. "Although Urchin did the swimming. I just rode on his back."

"Why?" Pearl asked.

To Marnie's surprise, her aunt blushed. "Reasons," she said vaguely. She clicked her fingers. "Garbo! Come!"

The Radio SeaWave studio was tucked deep inside a rocky outcrop, brightly lit by several angler fish and a large rock-crystal chandelier. Beautiful sea flowers grew on the uneven walls, blowing about in the gentle current. There was a mixing desk set at one end, a long table covered in Christabel Blue merchandise, and a recording booth with a sea-sponge microphone and shell headphones. Posters of Christabel lined the walls.

Two mermen with long beards—one green and one blue—looked up from the mixing desk as Garbo swam to a comfortable crystal bowl lined with sea moss below her very own poster and settled down.

"Cutting it close as usual, Christabel," said the merman with the green beard. "Hey, Marnie."

"Hi Sam," said Marnie. "This is my friend Pearl. Pearl, this is Sam, and the guy with the blue beard is Flip." Flip gave a slow smile, showing a gold tooth.

Christabel waved at the heaps of demo recordings lying around the room in teetering piles. "The music you want is probably in there somewhere," she said. She ran her fingers through her glossy blonde hair in a distracted way. "Now, where did I put today's playlist?"

As Christabel went through her soundchecks with Flip and Sam, Marnie and Pearl started working through the heaps of demos, trying to find Orla's sister's recording. Some of the demos had no names on them. Some had photographs on the front, and some had brightly colored titles. One mermaid had stuck lots of tiny shimmering shells all over the case, which made the name difficult to read.

"Ten seconds to recording," said Flip.

Christabel went inside the soundproof recording booth. Marnie and Pearl listened as the familiar theme music blasted around the room, and her famous introduction wafted out of the speakers in the rocky studio.

"I'm Christabel Blue and this is my *Big Blue Show*. All the tunes! All the fun! All the fish! And a special *Big Blue Show* hello to Pearl Cockle, who is visiting the studio tonight."

 84

Pearl squealed, knocking over the nearest pile of demos in shock. Marnie gave Aunt Christabel a thumbs-up. Her aunt really was the coolest person.

The show played a good mix of songs, and Christabel's jokes and funny stories flowed as continuously as the water around them. Pearl and Marnie listened and sang along as they worked through the demos, sifting through the definitely-nots and setting aside the maybes. Sheela's demo had to be here somewhere. It had to.

Pearl sat up suddenly. "Ooh, 'Love Underwater.' This is my favorite part of the show."

"Loved up or let down?" Christabel was saying. "'Love Underwater' is your chance to tell us all how you're feeling. Now, I've received a scallop from Leilani. Hi Leilani! Leilani wants to know: is it normal to cry crystal tears after a break-up? More after this tune."

"If it's true love, crystal tears are totally normal," said Pearl, as a well-known love song called "Eels and Feels" started playing. "Well, that's what my grandma always says. Everyone thinks true love is easy, but it's not."

True love was also extremely rare, Marnie knew.

"Lucky Leilani," she said.

Pearl squinted at Christabel in the recording booth. "Do you think your aunt has ever been in love?"

Marnie thought about how Aunt Christabel had blushed at Pearl's question about the East Lagoon Rocks. "I don't know," she said, frowning. "She's never been married."

"That doesn't mean she hasn't been in love," said Pearl.

"Back to your question, Leilani," said Christabel as the song finished. "If you're crying crystal tears, you have something very special. Trust me. My advice? Don't lose it."

Marnie stared at Aunt Christabel through the glass window of the recording booth. Was there something sad in her aunt's voice, or was she just imagining it? She shook her head. Thinking about Aunt Christabel being in love was weird.

By the time the show reached the "Dance 'n' Dazzle" finale, there was just one pile of demos left. Christabel played one of her own hits, and Marnie and Pearl started dancing around the studio, laughing and stretching their tails and fins. Feeling the energy, Garbo got out of her bowl and swam very fast around the ceiling.

"Night night, sleep tight, don't let the reef sharks bite," said Christabel as the music died away. "Back tomorrow. Stay tuned, tuna fish! Over and out."

Sam played the closing titles. The *Big Blue Show* was over. But Sheela Finnegan's demo was still nowhere to be found.

# Chapter
# Nine

"I was thinking," said Marnie as she and Pearl swam together into school the next morning. "What if Aunt Christabel gave Sheela Finnegan a job?"

Pearl glanced at her. "You're super-weird," she said. "All you talk about is helping someone who hates you."

Marnie did her best to explain. "I know it's not my fault about Orla's sister, but I feel responsible. You saw how untidy Radio SeaWave was, right?"

"So many people sent me scallops last night, telling me they heard my name on the show," said Pearl dreamily. "Talk about squid goals!"

"I was thinking that maybe Aunt Christabel could hire Sheela Finnegan as her assistant," Marnie said. "That would bring Sheela back to Mermaid Lagoon. I know it's not the same as Aunt Christabel playing Sheela's song on the radio, but it's better than nothing."

"Great," said Pearl. "But you'll have to find her first. She's missing in the hurricane, remember?"

It took longer than normal to swim to her first class because so many mermaids stopped Pearl to ask about her shout-out. Marnie and Pearl arrived in the music classroom just as the attendance scallop was leaving.

"You're late!" said Miss Tangle crossly. "Sit!"

"Orla's not here again either," Dora whispered as Marnie and Pearl hastily settled into their seats. "Miss Tangle's in a really strange mood."

Marnie thought uneasily about the last time she'd seen Orla Finnegan, red-eyed and swimming alone into the depths of the lagoon. She raised her hand.

"Miss Tangle, is Orla OK?" she asked.

Lupita and Dora stopped whispering and looked at Marnie in surprise.

Miss Tangle wiped her forehead with a seaweed tissue. "I'm afraid I have something to tell you, girls. Nobody has seen Orla Finnegan since yesterday," she said.

There was a shocked silence. Then everyone started talking at once.

"Is she missing then?"

"Maybe a reef shark ate her!"

"Good riddance."

Miss Tangle blew her nose. "The moment her poor parents find Sheela, they lose Orla!"

Marnie found her voice. "Sheela isn't missing anymore?"

"Dear Sheela," said Miss Tangle, sniffing. "She had taken cover from the hurricane in an underwater cave, but the cave was blocked by fallen stones. They pulled her out last night."

"What about Orla's parents, Miss Tangle?" asked Pearl. "Don't they know where Orla is?"

Miss Tangle wept more loudly. "Orla's parents went to the Gulf of Mexico to help find Sheela," she sobbed. "They're out of contact. We've had search parties out for Orla all night, but they haven't seen fin nor scale of her."

Marnie was glad to hear Sheela was all right. But now Orla was lost, and no one knew where she was. Scary things swam around the lagoon at night. Everyone knew that.

"Miss Tangle, are the search parties going out again today?" she asked.

Miss Tangle's tentacles shook. "They have given up. Orla Finnegan is in Neptune's hands now. She's lost! Lost forever, I fear!"

Marnie's mind whirred. There was no way she was going to be able to concentrate on lessons today. Not with Orla missing. *Yes*, she thought firmly: *missing. She wasn't dead. She couldn't be.*

She had to do something.

"Pearl, we have to look for Orla!" she said urgently at the end of attendance.

"I knew you were going to say that," said Pearl with a sigh.

"We can miss the rest of the day," said Marnie. "Look in places the search parties didn't think of. We'll search the whole lagoon if we have to."

"The lagoon is massive," Pearl pointed out. "We'll never be able to search all of it by ourselves."

"But Orla is in danger!" Marnie wailed. "And I'm the reason she was so upset yesterday!"

"No you're not," argued Pearl. "There's no way we can search the whole lagoon by ourselves before it gets dark. We just can't swim that fast."

Marnie thought of Urchin. On his back, she could search the whole lagoon before nightfall. But was she brave enough to try and ride him?

"We need to find Mr. Splendid at the stables," she said. "Come on!"

"But it's oceanography now and we're dissecting mussels," began Pearl.

"You don't have to come with me." Marnie squared her shoulders. "But I'm going and you can't stop me."

She rushed out of the Music Cave and into the corridor, past groups of serious-looking teachers. A few mermaids were floating around, weeping. It was clear that everyone had already given up hope.

"Where are you going?" called Dora as Marnie swam past hurriedly.

"To find Orla!" Marnie shouted back.

A golden tail and a cloud of red hair appeared beside her.

"Not by yourself, you're not," said Pearl.

"Mr. Splendid?" Marnie called when she and Pearl reached the oyster-shell doors. "Mr. SPLENDID!"

Andrew and Sandy put their heads out and snorted at Marnie and Pearl. Typhoon banged irritably at the walls of his stall. Urchin put his head out of his stable and screamed for Marnie's attention.

"There's no one here," Pearl said, gazing around.

Marnie thought about what Mr. Splendid had said about Christabel borrowing Urchin sometimes. "We'll have to borrow the seahorses without his permission then," she said. "He won't mind. Not for this." She hoped that was true.

Urchin bellowed more loudly, battering at his stable door. Marnie swam over and scratched him between the eyes, enjoying the feel of his cold scales under her fingers. Never in a million years had she thought she'd actually like a seahorse. But there was something about Urchin that was different.

"He looks friendly," said Pearl, swimming over.

Urchin shrieked and lunged at Pearl, snapping at her so fast that he almost caught the end of her nose.

"Don't do that, Urchin!" Marnie scolded, and Urchin bowed his head.

"Wow! How did you do that?" asked Pearl, impressed. "I thought you were scared of seahorses."

"I don't know," Marnie said. "Apparently he loved Aunt Christabel and now he seems to love me too. You try Andrew, Pearl. He's the green one over there. He won't bite."

Marnie found a bridle and saddle hanging on the

wall of Urchin's stall and fitted them to his slim blue body. She hoped she had them on the right way. Then she climbed on. Urchin snorted at her and fluttered his fins as she nervously guided him out of the stall. Pearl was waiting, perched on Andrew's back and holding on tightly to a pair of silvery reins.

"Let's go," Marnie said, with more confidence than she felt.

Urchin rocketed forward. Marnie bent down close to his blue neck, clinging on as best she could.

"Where to?" Pearl called through the rushing sound of the water.

"No idea!" Marnie shouted back.

Andrew swam steadily, bobbing his head backward and forward and snapping at the tiny krill that floated past. Urchin was a different matter. He strained and snorted and pulled so hard at his bridle that Marnie felt like her arms were going to fall off.

"We won't get lost if we follow that reef," Pearl suggested as they approached a ridged section of brightly colored coral.

*What were they doing?* Marnie thought a little hopelessly. The lagoon was so big. They didn't know where the search parties had looked, and they didn't have a map. Orla could be anywhere. Even inside a—

"Grey reef shark!" Pearl shouted suddenly.

Urchin snorted in shock as a silvery shark came out from behind the coral, sniffing at them with his flat nose. They raced away from the reef, Andrew almost level with Urchin. Marnie's heart was beating so quickly she thought it would crash out of her chest.

"Is the sh-sh-shark following us?" she stammered after a few minutes.

"No," Pearl said. She sounded a little disappointed.

This was a part of the lagoon that Marnie had never visited. She almost forgot about Orla as she gazed around.

"Coral trout," Pearl told her as they swam through shoals of beautiful flickering orange fish. Several huge creatures flew gracefully over their heads, their wide wings blocking the sunlight that filtered through the water. "And those are mantas," said Pearl. "There are some bluefin tuna over there too."

Marnie watched the tuna skim away into the distance.

"You know so much," she said.

"I'm a fish-spotter," Pearl admitted, turning a little pink. "It's not a very cool hobby, I know."

"I think it's awesome," said Marnie.

"I have a chart of all the fish I've spotted at home." Pearl beamed. "I'll show you one day." Her voice suddenly changed. "Hey, what's that?"

Marnie tore her eyes away from an octopus scooting along the lagoon bed below them. She stared. Letters had been carved into the surface of a rock just ahead of them.

"C-H-R-I . . ." She spelled out carefully. "Christabel! Pearl, it says Christabel!"

There were two more words.

"L-O-V-E-S A-R-T-H-U-R," Pearl spelled out. "Christabel loves Arthur. Who's Arthur?"

Marnie's aunt had never mentioned anyone called

Arthur. Puzzled, Marnie reached down and touched the letters, worn smooth by the current of the lagoon. "I don't know," she said.

"Maybe it's a different Christabel," Pearl said.

Urchin gave a sudden snort and took off. His scaly neck stretched out and his fins beat furiously.

"What's the rush?" Pearl shouted, chasing after Marnie as she held on tight.

"I think Urchin knows where we are," Marnie shouted back. "He must have been here before."

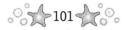

A great set of rocks were looming ahead of them, lit by the watery sun. The rugged shadows fell at a strange angle. *East*, Marnie thought.

The realization settled in her belly like a cold, hard stone.

They were at the East Lagoon Rocks.

# Chapter Ten

The East Lagoon Rocks! Human divers had seen Aunt Christabel at this place. What if someone saw Marnie and Pearl?

"Pearl," Marnie hissed. "We can't be here, we—"

An odd noise filtered towards them. Marnie stopped talking. She'd heard that sound before.

"Someone's crying," said Pearl, trying to stop Andrew from eating the seaweed on the rockface.

"Orla," Marnie gasped.

It had to be. Of all the places in Mermaid Lagoon, Orla Finnegan had come here.

Marnie rode Urchin around the rocks, trying to figure out where the crying was coming from. The rocks were almost smooth, with very few crags wherea crying mermaid could hide. Urchin snuffled and snorted and pulled eagerly.

"You brought Aunt Christabel here, didn't you?" said Marnie, realizing. "That's why you know it! Come on then, Urchin. Where is Orla?"

She loosened the reins. Urchin took off, flying up close to the surface of the water. And then Marnie spotted it: a gaping black hole covered with weeds. The crying sounded louder here.

Marnie swam up to the hole. "Hello?" she called into the blackness.

The crying stopped. Orla's voice was faint but filled with hope. "Who's there?"

"It's Marnie!" She peered more closely into the tunnel. "Where are you?"

"Marnie?" Orla sounded wary now. "What are you doing here?"

"We're rescuing you, you idiot," Pearl said, swimming over to join Marnie at the tunnel mouth.

"Why?"

"Is this really the time for questions?" Pearl demanded.

A sob and a hiccup echoed towards them. "I didn't want to go home in case my parents had bad news. I love my sister so much. I've been so worried about her ever since she went to the Gulf of Mexico and now all my worries have come true. So I came here and swam up the tunnel. Sheela told me once that this is a good place to hide when you want to be by yourself."

Marnie had always thought that it was only Aunt Christabel who had come here. Now it sounded like she was just the only mermaid who had gotten caught.

Orla was still talking. "But I'm cold and tired now and I want to go home even if there's bad news, except I can't because—"

"Orla," Marnie interrupted. "Listen to me. They found your sister."

Orla made a funny sound. "They found her? Really? Is she OK?"

"She's fine."

Orla started crying again.

"So you can come out now," said Pearl in a practical sort of voice.

"I can't—"

"Everything's OK," Marnie said. "And we have to get back to school."

"But that's what I'm trying to tell you. I CAN'T come out!" Orla wailed. "There's an eel—"

Suddenly a huge, ugly head darted into view from the tunnel mouth, its fangs glinting. Urchin bucked in surprise, and Marnie squealed.

"Ooh, a moray," said Pearl. "Did you know they have two sets of jaws?"

Marnie didn't want to think about two sets of jaws. One was bad enough.

There was no way Orla could swim past the eel without being eaten.

"Where are you exactly, Orla?" she said, from a safer distance.

They heard Orla sniffing. "There's a pool up here on the surface and I'm sitting in it. I don't know what to do!"

"You'll have to get out of the pool and jump off the rocks," Marnie said. "Get back into the water that way."

"But I'll lose my voice if I get out of the water!" Orla wailed back. "I'll lose my tail!"

Without hesitation, Marnie made a decision.

"Watch out for boats, Pearl," she said, sliding off Urchin. "I'm going up to the surface. Let me know if anyone's coming."

"No!" shouted Pearl. "You can't do that. What if someone sees you?"

Marnie ignored her. With a strong flip of her tail, she

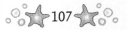

took off towards the rippling surface. She'd never put her head above water before. Mermaids can breathe air, so she wasn't scared about that. But she was scared of human divers. And boats.

Pearl was right. What if she came face to face with a human?

But what if she left Orla there, and she got eaten by the eel? There was only one thing to do. She had to be brave.

Marnie burst through the surface of the water. The heat of the sun hit her face and the air in her lungs was hot and unfamiliar. She practiced breathing for a while, staying low in the water, and gazed at the view. She had no idea the lagoon was so flat.

The East Lagoon rocks were pale pink in the heat of the sun. Nothing grew on them.

"Orla?" Marnie called as loudly as she dared, swimming around the shore.

She spotted Orla's dark head near a pale pink beach on the north side of the rocks. There was a pool, just

as Orla had said. Orla was sitting in it, her eyes wide and frightened.

"It's not far to the edge," Marnie called from the water in her most encouraging voice. "Just climb out of the pool and come toward me. You probably won't even have time to lose your tail."

"But what if I do?" Orla cried. "I'll never be able to swim again! And I don't want to lose my voice!"

Marnie thought of Queen Maretta striding out of the water to meet the Weathermaker. *She* must have got her tail back. You couldn't be Queen of the Mermaids without a tail. Or a voice. Could you?

"I'll do it if you will," Marnie said.

Orla gave a shaky smile. "That's what you said at the stables. I'm sorry about everything, Marnie. I've been so angry and worried . . ."

"It's okay. We'll figure it out," said Marnie. "Let's just get you out of here first."

"Thank you for coming to find me," said Orla.

"Of course." Marnie smiled. "Now are you ready?"

Orla nodded.

Before she could talk herself out of it, Marnie pulled herself ashore. And she watched her fins and scales vanish. Smooth pale skin replaced them and Marnie gawked as legs and feet appeared. She wiggled her toes.

*Weird*, she said to herself. Only nothing came out when she said it.

Marnie froze. No tail. No voice. What was she doing?

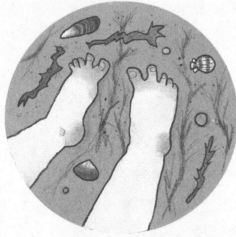

She was standing on the East Lagoon Rocks like a human. She wasn't a mermaid anymore. This was bonkers!

Through her panic, Marnie felt cool fingers on her arm. Orla had climbed out of the pool and was standing beside her. Her legs were as pale as her anxious face.

*We did it,* she mouthed. *Now what?*

Marnie gripped Orla's hand. *We go home.*

They walked clumsily down the beach together. At that moment, a sparkle of sunlight hit the water, and it reminded her of something. She knew what happened to Sheela's demo: It had been at Radio SeaWave all along.

She had to get back to the studio and see if she was right. But only if she could change back into a mermaid.

Luckily, the moment Marnie's toes touched the water, they changed back into a powerful fin. She dived. Her tail flashed. The water felt like home.

"Neptune's knickers," said Orla beside her, her own purple tail restored. "I'm NEVER doing that again."

"Your voice is back!" Marnie gasped.

Orla laughed in relief. "So's yours!"

"And I know where Sheela's demo is. I know what happened! And we're going to fix it. Tonight!"

"Are we friends now?" said Orla, sounding a bit nervous.

Marnie grinned. "I guess we are."

Pearl swam over on Andrew. "Urchin keeps teasing the moray eel by sticking his head in the tunnel. I think

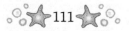

they know each other. Listen, loads of fish swam this way a minute ago, like they were swimming away from something. I think humans must be near."

Suddenly Marnie heard a noise in the distance. A boat. She grabbed Urchin's bridle. "Time to go, Urchin. Can you carry two of us?"

Urchin lunged at Orla, his teeth bared. Despite Marnie's best efforts, he refused to let Orla anywhere near him, so Pearl offered Orla a seat on Andrew instead.

"Thanks, Pearl." Orla blushed. "I'm sorry I called you a flounder-face, by the way."

"Don't mention it, sea slug," said Pearl. She grinned. "Just kidding."

They dived as deep as they could go. Marnie let Urchin lead, trusting that he knew the way back. As they passed the rock carved with *CHRISTABEL LOVES ARTHUR,* she wondered again. *Who was Arthur?*

# The Last Chapter

Sheela Finnegan's demo recording sat on the table in front of Marnie, Orla, Pearl, and Christabel in the Radio SeaWave studio. Sheela had decorated it with tiny mother-of-pearl fragments, and it sparkled in the light. Several other sparkly things sat beside it: some delicate crystal beads, a bangle, and a beautiful shell.

"Garbo?" Christabel said. "Explain yourself."

Garbo was sulking in her bowl underneath her poster. All the sparkly things that she'd stolen had been taken from her sea-moss bed, and she wasn't happy about it.

"You could have ruined a promising career," Christabel scolded. "Orla, please tell your sister that I'll play her demo on tonight's show, with apologies for my thieving goldfish."

"Thank you so much," Orla said eagerly. "My sister will be really happy."

"She won't be rich and famous right away," Christabel warned. "The music business is tough. But her demo is good and if she works hard, she could make it in a year or two."

The smile fell from Orla's face. "She has to keep working in the Gulf of Mexico for another year?" she said in dismay. "But the hurricanes—"

"Auntie, could you give Sheela a job in your studio?" Marnie begged. "You said you needed an assistant."

Christabel looked doubtful. "It isn't very glamorous work."

"Sheela won't mind," Orla said quickly. "She would love working with you. She thinks you're incredible." She blushed. "So do I."

"It's decided then," said Aunt Christabel, flicking her tail and rising from the table with Sheela's demo in her hand. "Send a message to the Gulf of Mexico and bring your sister back at once. She can start work right away. NO, Garbo. No treats tonight."

"Thank you, Marnie!" Orla cried as Christabel swam off with Flip and Sam to get ready for the evening show. She threw her arms around Marnie and hugged her tightly. "You're the most amazing mermaid in the world."

Marnie blushed. "I just wanted to help," she said.

"That's what makes you amazing," Orla said, squeezing Marnie's hands tight.

"I'm sorry I've been so mean to you."

"I forgive you."

Pearl was examining the shell, bangle, and crystal beads that were still on the table. Garbo watched mournfully.

"Marnie, you know you said you didn't think your aunt had ever been in love?" Pearl said.

*CHRISTABEL LOVES ARTHUR.* The words on the lagoon rock came back into Marnie's mind. She still hadn't asked Aunt Christabel about it.

"Yes?" she said, doubtfully.

Pearl looked triumphant. "Well, she has. And it was true love."

"How do you know?" asked Marnie in surprise.

Pearl held out her hand. The tiny beads in her palm looked like little drops of water. Marnie stared.

"Leaping lobsters!" said Orla. "Those are crystal tears!"

"And I think Garbo found them here in Christabel's studio," said Pearl.

"I'm Christabel Blue and this is my *Big Blue Show*," Christabel said as the title music faded. "All the tunes! All the fun! All the FISH!"

Dolphinitely
The Last
Chapter

The sun was blinding on the water of the lagoon, bouncing off the waves and dazzling Arthur Bagshot through his binoculars. He lowered them and rubbed his eyes.

The boat's first mate put his head out of the cabin. "Anything, boss?"

Arthur thought he had seen something by the East Lagoon Rocks a few hours earlier. Two tails, one pink and one purple, flashing through the water. Maybe they were dolphins. Maybe they weren't. Looking at the same rocks for ten years was enough to drive anyone bananas.

"No," he said. "Nothing."

"Enough for today then?"

Arthur ran his hands through his hair. "Yes, enough for today."

"Back tomorrow?"

Arthur polished the lenses on the binoculars with the sleeve of his shirt.

"Why not?" he said.

After all, he always came back.

Just in case.

FIN

## About the Author

**Lucy Courtenay** has worked on a number of series for young readers, as well as books for young adults. When not writing, she enjoys singing, reading, and traveling. She lives in Farnham, England, with her husband, her two sons, and a cat named Crumbles.

## About the Illustrator

**Sheena Dempsey** is a children's book illustrator and author from Cork, Ireland, who was shortlisted for the Sainsbury's Book Award. She lives in London with her partner, Mick, and her retired racing greyhound, Sandy.